The Trouble with Gnomes

'The Trouble with Gnomes'
An original concept by Jenny Jinks
© Jenny Jinks

Illustrated by Carolina Coroa

Published by MAVERICK ARTS PUBLISHING LTD

Studio 11, City Business Centre, 6 Brighton Road,

Horsham, West Sussex, RH13 5BB

© Maverick Arts Publishing Limited November 2020

+44 (0)1403 256941

A CIP catalogue record for this book is available at the British Library.

ISBN 978-1-84886-731-4

www.maverickbooks.co.uk

This book is rated as: Brown Band (Guided Reading)

The Trouble with Gnomes

Written by
Jenny Jinks

Illustrated by
Carolina Coroa

Chapter 1

"Found you!" Hettie cried to her best friend Maddie, as she jumped around a bush. But Hettie's long legs got in a tangle, and she landed in a bundle on top of Maddie, who had been trying her best to hide.

"Hettie, get off me!" Maddie mumbled from under the heap.

"Sorry," Hettie said, trying to untangle herself so they could get up. Hettie was always landing in a heap. The trouble was her legs were just a little bit too long, like two long strands of spaghetti, and

Hettie couldn't always control them.

"My turn to hide," said Hettie.

Maddie closed her eyes and began to count while Hettie searched for somewhere new to hide. Behind the dustbins? No, she had hidden there yesterday. In the portaloo? No way, she had been in there before and it was much too stinky. Hettie spotted their favourite climbing tree. She could hide in its branches. That was one good thing about having long legs:

she could get right into the top branches where her friends couldn't.

Hettie started to climb. She put her foot on a thin branch but it snapped. Hettie tried to grab hold of the tree, but it was too late. She started to fall. But for some strange reason, she didn't hit the ground. She just kept on falling. It felt like the ground was swallowing her up!

Down and down she fell, until finally she landed...

THUD!

Then everything went black.

Chapter 2

Hettie opened her eyes. What had happened? Where was she?

She was lying on her back somewhere dark and gloomy. There was light far above her—the sky. She must have fallen down a hole. Maybe it was a sink hole. She had learnt about those at school. Sometimes the earth suddenly opened up, making a huge hole in the ground, and swallowing anything in its way. This was so cool! Except for the fact that she was covered in dirt, and had a really bad pain in her head where she had hit it in the fall.

Hettie tried to stand up, but when she moved she felt dizzy so she lay back down again. Hettie looked around. There were little tunnels all around her, leading in all directions. *That's odd*, Hettie thought. Maybe something lived down there. A rabbit perhaps. Or a badger.

Then Hettie heard a sound. It rumbled right through the ground, getting louder and nearer.

Was it an earthquake? Was the ground about to swallow Hettie up again? Or collapse in on top of her?

Hettie squeezed her eyes shut, preparing for the worst. The noise grew louder and louder. The ground shook underneath her.

And then, just as suddenly as it had started, the rumbling stopped.

Hettie peeked out through one eye... and then shut it again quickly. She must have hit her head harder than she thought. She opened an eye again, then the other one.

A hundred pairs of tiny eyes glowed back at her in the darkness. They were peering out of little round grubby faces, and they were staring straight at her. It hadn't been an earthquake. It was feet. Lots of them.

Hettie was surrounded by tiny people.

Chapter 3

Hettie blinked. Then blinked again. Surely she must be dreaming. Just how hard had she hit her head?

But she could no longer just see them, she could feel them too. Hundreds of tiny hands, poking and prodding all around her, until suddenly she was being lifted up off the ground.

"Stop! Get off me," cried Hettie. "HELP! I'm being kidnapped!"

But nobody could hear her down the sink hole, and the tiny people did not stop. They carried Hettie off down one of the tiny tunnels.

Hettie tried her best to break free, but the little people were surprisingly strong, and the tunnels were so small. There was hardly room for her to blink, let alone make a run for it. Hettie was bumped, and knocked, and scraped along the tunnel as the funny little people carried her along.

At long last, they came to a stop. Hettie was dumped on the hard floor.

She got up quickly, before anyone could try to pick her up again, but then she bumped her head on the ceiling, so she had to crouch back down.

They were in a big chamber, much like where Hettie had landed. But even though it was much bigger than the tunnels, it still was not nearly tall enough for Hettie and her longs legs. She had to fold herself up awkwardly to make herself fit.

Once she had finally sorted herself out, she noticed what was in front of her. A large throne had been made out of earth. Another of the strange little people was sitting on it. He was covered from head to toe in colourful robes, and a golden crown sat on his head. He was clearly the little people's king.

The king looked down on Hettie with a mysterious smile. All the other little people stared up at Hettie, too, their eyes wide. It was only now that Hettie got a really good look at them. They were small, perhaps only a foot tall. They looked just like very small people, but with very round noses, and big rosy red cheeks, and they all had long beards. They looked oddly familiar, as though she had seen them somewhere before. Hettie stared back at them all. She couldn't help but wonder what was going to happen next. Were they going to lock her up? Torture her? *Eat* her?!

But then something happened that Hettie could not have predicted even in a million years.

"Our hero has arrived," the king announced.

"Ooooooh!" the others all said. And then, before she could stop them, they were lifting Hettie up and cheering loudly.

Not again, thought Hettie as she was bounced about on their shoulders. She stared round at them all in confusion. What on earth was going on?

Chapter 4

"There must be some sort of mistake," said Hettie, when they finally put her back down. "I'm no hero."

"Oh, but of course you are," the king said, smiling at her. "We knew someone brave and strong would be sent to save us. And here you are."

"But... I haven't been sent to you. I just fell down a hole. I fall a lot," Hettie tried to explain.

But nobody was listening.

"Our hero has come from above," the king told everyone.

"Ooooh!" they all said again, and started chatting excitedly.

Hettie couldn't take it any longer.

"I'm sorry," she said loudly over the chatter. She tried to stand up again, but could only manage to crouch. "There has been a super massive mistake. I am not a hero. I am not brave, or strong. And I have definitely not been sent here from above to save a load of... what even are you, anyway?"

"We are gnomes," the king said.

"Gnomes?" Hettie tried not to laugh. "Like the ones in people's gardens?" So that was why they looked familiar.

"Those garden gnomes guard the entrance to my kingdom," the king replied. "That is how we know danger is coming. That is why you were sent to us. We need your help."

Hettie looked at all the hopeful faces staring up at her. Maybe they really did need her help. Either way, it didn't look like they were going to take no for an answer.

"Okay," she said finally. "I'll do my best."

Chapter 5

The king wasted no time in getting Hettie ready for battle.

"Let's see what sort of warrior you are. Choose your weapon," the king said. "Do you prefer a sword? Axe? Fishing rod?"

Hettie had never used any of them before. But a sword sounded alright. A large gnome called Gnorm handed her a sword—although in Hettie's hand it looked more like a toothpick. Everyone waited, looking at Hettie. What was she supposed to do with it?

She tried twirling it in her hand, but she accidentally dropped it. Some gnomes at the back of the group sniggered. Hettie quickly picked it back up. She tried lunging with it, like she had seen knights do, but she nearly lost her balance.

The group were starting to murmur and fidget. Hettie didn't want them to think she was completely rubbish. She thought quickly. She had played darts with her dad in their garage. The tiny sword was about the same size...

She picked a point on the wall, and threw the sword as hard as she could. It whooshed through the air and hit the wall with a loud...

TWANG!

"Oooooh!" the gnomes all said, finally looking impressed.

"Very good," the king nodded. "Now it's time for the real training to begin."

Gnorm took Hettie to get kitted out. He was big and looked tough and brave, like a real warrior. Not like Hettie, who just always looked a bit awkward. Gnorm got her some armour which was about ten sizes too small. They attached the largest shields they could find, which would just have to do, and he found her a slightly bigger war hammer. Nobody could get the sword out of the wall.

They did lots of training. Hettie really wasn't very good. Her super long limbs always seemed to get in the way, and she kept dropping the war hammer.

"Can we take a break?" Hettie asked. She was exhausted.

"No. We can't stop yet. We have a lot of work to

do. But don't worry, you are getting there." Gnorm smiled kindly at her. "By the time the beasts arrive, I am sure you will be ready."

Beasts? Had Hettie heard that right? Exactly what kind of danger was she expected to fight? And why hadn't she thought to ask that question before she had agreed to help?!

Chapter 6

"B-b-beasts?!" Hettie stuttered. "What do you mean 'beasts'?"

"There is an army of enormous hairy beasts coming this way.

They have huge pointy teeth like knives, and long sharp claws like daggers. And they will be here any minute."

Any minute? But Hettie wasn't anywhere near ready to fight an army of huge hairy monsters! What was she going to do?

"Ummm, I just need to use the toilet," Hettie said.

"Okay," said Gnorm. "But hurry back. We haven't much time."

Hettie rushed away along one of the winding tunnels. She had no idea where she was going. All she knew was that she had to get out of there. She was no warrior. She was a clumsy scaredy-cat. The gnomes would be better off without her.

Hettie was getting more and more lost in the maze of tunnels. It was hopeless. She was never going to find her way out. She would be stuck down there forever. Then she spotted something glowing in a patch of sunlight ahead. It was her school lunch bag! She must have dropped it when she fell down the hole. She had found her way back. She could go home!

Hettie was about to climb out of the hole when she heard a deep rumbling behind her, getting louder and louder.

Oh no, the gnomes! They were coming to get her!

Except, this sounded different. The rumbling was deeper, and louder. The beast army—it was coming!

Hettie froze. What should she do? She was so close to escaping. Just a short climb and she could run back home and forget this ever happened.

But the gnomes were counting on her. They needed a hero. And right now, Hettie was the only hero they had.

Hettie took a deep breath, adjusted her armour, put her lunch bag on her back, and hurried towards the terrifying sound.

Chapter 7

Hettie found her way back to the main chamber surprisingly quickly. The tunnels weren't so difficult once you got used to them, and she just followed the sound of thundering footsteps.

When she got back to the main hall, the gnomes were getting ready for battle, but they all looked terrified. When the king saw Hettie, he jumped up from his throne.

"I told you our hero wouldn't abandon us," he said.

Suddenly the noise got much louder. All the gnomes jumped, and quickly found something to hide behind.

Hettie stood there, alone. She told herself that she was brave. She was a warrior. A hero. And she almost believed herself. Almost.

The wall in front of her started to shake. The army was about to break through.

Just as the wall was about to crumble, Gnorm jumped up and stood beside her. He held his axe up at the ready.

"Took a long time to find the toilets, did it?" he muttered.

Hettie looked at him and blushed. "Something like that," she said.

There was another loud **CRASH** as something hit the other side of the wall. Gnorm and Hettie nodded to each other. Whatever was coming, they would face it together.

The last bit of wall finally cracked, and crumbled away. Hettie took a deep breath as through the wall burst an army of...

RABBITS? Hettie was confused. From beyond the crumbled down wall, dozens of cute, snuffling, fluffy bunnies hopped around her.

The gnomes squeaked, and hid further down in their hiding spots. She could tell Gnorm was shaking beside her. Hettie kept her war hammer up ready. The army must be coming just behind. But nothing else came. Where was the army of fearsome beasts?

These weren't fearsome beasts. They were cute little fluffy bunnies!

She laughed as the bunnies lopped into the hall. She turned to see the gnomes all looking more terrified than ever. Every time a rabbit hopped closer, the gnomes shrunk further into their boots, shaking with fear.

Then Hettie realised. The rabbits might be tiny and cute to her, but to the little gnomes they would be huge and terrifying.

Gnorm held his axe up bravely, ready to charge. Hettie didn't want the rabbits to get hurt.

They didn't mean any harm.

If only there was some way she could lead them away from the gnome kingdom so everyone would be safe. And then she had an idea.

"WAIT!" she shouted. Everyone stopped and looked at her. Even the rabbits stopped in surprise. "I know how to get rid of these fluffy bu—I mean, fearsome beasts. Nobody needs to get hurt."

Chapter 8

Hettie opened her lunch bag and took out the pot of untouched vegetable sticks her dad insisted on giving her every day. She held out a carrot stick.

The rabbits all hopped towards her. They sniffed it excitedly.

Slowly, Hettie backed along the tunnel. Her plan was working. All the rabbits were following her.

Hettie lead them all the way through the tunnels until she came to the sink hole. She climbed out, and then lifted each of them up and out of the hole. Then she took them to a nearby field. She was sure they would enjoy their new home, full of long juicy grass to eat. She gave them each a vegetable stick, just to make sure they wouldn't come back in a hurry. She promised herself she would come back and feed them every day to make sure they stayed away from the gnomes.

Hettie headed back to the sink hole. All the gnomes were there, waiting for her. They cheered

when they saw her coming.

"Our hero," the king said. They all bowed down to her, even the king. Hettie blushed. She still didn't feel much like a hero. She was just plain old Hettie, the clumsy girl with legs too long. But she was happy that she had been able to help.

"How can we ever thank you?" the king of the gnomes asked.

"You don't need to do anything," Hettie said. "It was nothing, really."

"We owe you. If you ever need anything, you only have to ask. We will never be far away," the king said.

Hettie blushed again. She felt sad leaving the gnomes. But it was starting to get late, and her parents would be getting worried.

"I have to go now. But thanks for believing in me.

I've never been a hero before. I hope we will see each other again sometime," Hettie said.

"Oh, you can count on it," the king said, smiling mysteriously.

"Bye," she said, and she turned and walked home, wondering if she would ever see the gnomes again.

★★★

The next morning, Hettie and Maddie walked to school together. The adventures of the previous day already felt like a dream.

"Where did you get to last night?" Maddie asked. "I looked for you for ages before I gave up and went home! You must have found an awesome hiding place."

"You wouldn't believe me even if I told you,"

Hettie said, smiling to herself.

"Hey, is it just me, or have loads of gnomes suddenly popped up in everyone's gardens?" Maddie said. Hettie had noticed them too. And there were a few familiar faces among them. "I think they're a bit weird, don't you?"

"Actually, I think they are pretty cool once you get to know them," Hettie said, secretly smiling down at one in a nearby garden. And, unnoticed by anyone else, Gnorm winked back at her.

Discussion Points

1. How did Hettie find the gnome kingdom at the beginning of the story?

2. What were the enormous hairy beasts that the gnomes were afraid of?

a) Bunnies

b) Wolves

c) Cats

3. What was your favourite part of the story?

4. How did Hettie defeat the beasts and save the gnomes?

5. Why do you think the gnomes were scared of the beasts when Hettie wasn't?

6. Who was your favourite character and why?

7. There were moments in the story when Hettie had to be **brave**. Where do you think the story shows this most?

8. What do you think happens after the end of the story?

Book Bands for Guided Reading

The Institute of Education book banding system is a scale of colours that reflects the various levels of reading difficulty. The bands are assigned by taking into account the content, the language style, the layout and phonics. Word, phrase and sentence level work is also taken into consideration.

The Maverick Readers Scheme is a bright, attractive range of books covering the pink to grey bands. All of these books have been book banded for guided reading to the industry standard and edited by a leading educational consultant.

To view the whole Maverick Readers scheme, visit our website at

www.maverickearlyreaders.com

Or scan the QR code to view our scheme instantly!

Maverick Chapter Readers
(From Lime to Grey Band)

Pink

Red

Yellow

Blue

Green

Orange

Turquoise

Purple

Gold

White

Lime

Brown

Grey